Harriet
Follows Her
Heart

by Wendy Hornik

Illustrated by Miranda Allard

Dedication

This book is dedicated to my grandmother, Harriet Benedyk, who taught me to listen to that voice deep inside my heart, and to my beautiful daughter, Annie Hornik, who has been dancing for fourteen years. She moves with such grace and beauty and has a smile that lights up the stage.

Published by Orange Hat Publishing 2023
PB ISBN: 9781645384793
HC ISBN: 9781645384786

orangehatpublishing.com

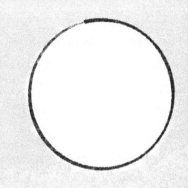

Harriet was a hippo who did many *ordinary* things but dreamt about doing **extraordinary** things. During the hot African days, she and the other young hippos would lounge in a small water hole while their parents rested in a large pond.

At night, she would go up onto the land with her family, where her mother and father would farm for food, and she would attend Hippopotamus School.

At school, Harriet would learn how to...

swim,

dive,

and garden.

After school, she would go to the water hole, where she sat around and watched other hippo kids basking in the water, all the while knowing that something wasn't quite right.

Most hippos usually ended up becoming doctors, teachers, or farmers, but Harriet had different thoughts and dreams. Harriet didn't want to be like everybody else. She yearned to make people happy, to warm their hearts by twirling and leaping as the very first hippo dancer.

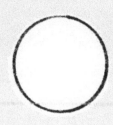

When Harriet told her parents about her dream, they chuckled and said, "Hippos don't dance. Have you ever looked at how short your legs are?"

Harriet looked at her legs and thought, *I know they're short, but they are the only legs I have, and they want to dance.*

Harriet danced to school that night. "I love to dance," she whispered to the moon.

There, Harriet's teacher asked the students what they dreamt about being when they grew up. She responded dreamily, "A dancer."

The other students began to giggle. Then her teacher said, "Harriet, that is a neat idea, but hippos don't dance."

Harriet quietly mumbled,
"But that is my dream."

Her teacher shook her head.

After school, Harriet told her grandmother about her dream, expecting her to react as everyone else had. However, Harriet was surprised by her grandmother's response. She said, "You do what your **heart** tells you to do! Your **heart** will always lead you in the right direction."

Harriet looked puzzled and asked, "What do you mean?"

"When you have a deep desire in your **heart** to do something, you need to put all your effort into it. You may get tired, and people may discourage you, but you have to keep trying."

That night, Harriet decided she would go
after her dream. She carefully crafted
a plan that she hoped would help her
become a fabulous hippo dancer.

So instead of lounging in the water hole during the day, she secretly watched the pink flamingos, or the Pinkies as they were called, from behind a mound near their wading pool.

THE PLAN

ME!

The Pinkies were widely known as the best dancers in Africa.

Then, Harriet would go home and try to imitate their beautiful movements. In the beginning, she struggled.

Many times, she tumbled into a pile.

But she remembered the words of her grandmother,

"You may get tired, and people may discourage you, but you have to keep trying," and she would try and try until she mastered the skill.

After Harriet had practiced for months and months, she felt confident enough to ask the Pinkies if she could join their dancing group. At first, the other flamingos looked at Harriet and laughed because of her short legs and round body, but then the smallest, kindest flamingo stepped up.

"Remember when you
thought I was too little to join, but you
gave me a chance and realized how lovely my leaps
were?" They all nodded in agreement
and decided to let Harriet try out.

When the flamingos put on their music and Harriet began to dance, she did a perfect chassé and beautiful pirouette. The flamingos could not believe their eyes. Harriet looked so magical and graceful. The Pinkies unanimously agreed to have her not only be part of the team but also to have her be the star of their upcoming show.

When word spread across the continent about a hippo dancing with the Pinkies, every animal was surprised that a hippo could fit in with the flamingos, but none more than the hippos themselves. The hippos who had teased and laughed at Harriet began to wonder if maybe, just maybe, they had been wrong.

THE PINKIES
STARRING HARRIET

Pinkies Theater
August 6

On the opening night of their show, herds of
animals flocked to the flamingos' theater and stood
in line to get a ticket to see Harriet. Many animals
still doubted that she could dance and even made
jokes while standing in line.

But as the curtain opened and the lights came on, there was Harriet in the middle of all the flamingos in her pink tutu. She was the centerpiece of the entire show. As the group began to dance, everyone sat in awe because they could not believe how amazing she was. She may not have had the elegance of a gazelle or the speed of a cheetah, but she had her own hip-hip-hippo style that made her beautiful to watch.

When the music slowly faded and Harriet did her final curtsy, the entire crowd rose and gave her a standing ovation. It was the most successful performance ever!

At the end of the show, the animals waited outside to congratulate her and said, "You were amazing! You inspired us to follow our **hearts** and go after our dreams!"

When Harriet arrived back at home, her grandmother quietly whispered in her ear, "Always remember, your **HEART** will lead you in the right direction!"

Finale

Author Bio

As a middle school English and literature teacher and a mom of two amazing teenagers, Wendy loves sharing books that inspire children to be better people, follow their dreams, and be true to themselves. *Harriet Follows Her Heart* is written in memory of her grandmother, Harriet Benedyk. She inspired Wendy to be a better person and taught her not to let others' judgments stop her from following her dreams.

Illustrator Bio

Miranda, a former student of Wendy's, attends the University of Wisconsin - Parkside, double-majoring in art and marketing. She is passionate about using her artistic abilities to bring joy to people's hearts. In *Harriet Follows Her Heart*, that's exactly what Harriet dreams of doing through dancing. At eighteen, Miranda followed her dream and started an art and design business, Daffodil Blossoms. Miranda has often been told that she would be great at illustrating children's books, but she never thought she would have the chance to do it until now!

Printed in the USA
CPSIA information can be obtained
at www.ICGtesting.com
LVHW071732011123
762562LV00015B/774